Little Red
Robin

Lulu
and the Caterpillars

Do you have all the Little Red Robin books?

- [ ] Buster's Big Surprise
- [ ] The Purple Butterfly
- [ ] How Bobby Got His Pet
- [ ] We are Super!
- [ ] New Friends
- [ ] Robo-Robbie
- [ ] The Fleas Who Fight Crime
- [ ] A Friend for Dragon
- [ ] When the Tooth Fairy Forgot
- [ ] Silly Name for a Monster
- [ ] Princess Pip's Perfect Party
- [ ] Lulu and the Caterpillars

Also available as ebooks

If you feel ready to read a longer book,
look out for more stories about Lulu

Lulu
and the Caterpillars

Little Red
Robin

Hilary McKay

Illustrated by Priscilla Lamont

SCHOLASTIC

For Aditi, because you like the Lulu books!
With love from Hilary McKay

Scholastic Children's Books
An imprint of Scholastic Ltd
Euston House, 24 Eversholt Street
London, NW1 1DB, UK
Registered office: Westfield Road, Southam, Warwickshire, CV47 0RA
SCHOLASTIC and associated logos are trademarks and/or registered
trademarks of Scholastic Inc.

First published in the UK in 2014 by Scholastic Ltd

Text copyright © Hilary McKay, 2014
Illustrations © Priscilla Lamont, 2014

The rights of Hilary McKay and Priscilla Lamont
to be identified as the author and illustrator of
this work have been asserted by them.

ISBN 978 1407 13881 7

A CIP catalogue record for this book is available from the British Library

Printed in China.

1 3 5 7 9 10 8 6 4 2

www.scholastic.co.uk/zone

Chapter One

Lulu loved animals.

All sorts of animals.

Huge ones like elephants.

Small ones like ladybirds.

Dangly ones, climbing ones, furry ones, flying ones.

In Lulu's house there were no animals. There was Lulu and her mum and her dad.

"We could have a dog," said Lulu. "Or perhaps a cat, or some rabbits. Guinea pigs are lovely. We could have a hamster, or a lot of little mice."

"Hmm," said Lulu's mum and dad.

"Well," said Lulu, "would you like a parrot? I know someone with a parrot they don't want."

"Who would look after the parrot and the rabbits?" asked Lulu's mother. "Who would clean out the hamster and guinea pigs? Who would feed the cat and walk the dog and catch the mice when they escape?"

"Me," said Lulu.

"Perhaps one day," said Lulu's mum and dad.

3

Lulu's friends said, "That's what grown-ups always say."

Her friends didn't want animals, but they wanted other things.

Charlie wanted a James Bond car.

Henry wanted a drum kit.

Lulu's cousin Mellie wanted a hot-air balloon. She thought she could keep it tied to the roof.

"Hmm," said the grown-ups. "Perhaps one day."

Chapter Two

One day Lulu and Mellie and Charlie and Henry
were all in Lulu's garden. They were playing Chase.

First they chased Mellie up the tree. Then they chased Charlie into the bin. Then they chased Henry over the fence. Then they chased Lulu, but they couldn't catch her because she was the fastest.

They chased her round and round the garden
until she ran behind the shed.

Behind the shed were nettles.

"OW! OW! OW! OW! OW!"
cried Lulu.

Lulu's mum put cream on the nettle stings.

It made them a
little bit better.

Mellie hugged her.

Charlie let her borrow
the James Bond lunch
box his dad had bought
him instead of a car.

Henry gave her a
go on the recorder
his mum had
bought him instead
of a drum kit.

Later Lulu's dad came home and looked behind the shed. Then he cut down all the nettles and raked them into a heap.

Lulu and Mellie went to look at the heap.

"What's that?" asked Lulu.

Some of the nettle leaves were folded in a cobwebby tangle.

Something was moving inside. Lulu bent to look.

Small black
caterpillars were
wriggling there.

"Yuck! Yuck! Yuck!"
squealed Mellie, but Lulu
said, "What will they do,
now their nettles have
been cut down?"

Very gently, Lulu
lifted the cobwebby
tangle and put it in
Charlie's lunch box.

Chapter Three

There were twenty-seven hairy black caterpillars.

"I have twenty-seven pets now!" said Lulu proudly.

But. . .

The twenty-seven caterpillars did not want to live in Charlie's lunch box.

They did not want to live in a shoebox in Lulu's bedroom.

Or travel in the car in an ice-cream tub.

When Lulu took the caterpillars to Nan's
house, Nan found a giant plastic jam jar for
them. But they didn't want to stay in the jam jar.
While everyone was having lunch, the caterpillars
went exploring.

They were wild, wild caterpillars and they
wanted to be free.

All afternoon, Lulu tracked down caterpillars.
She scooped them up with leaves, so as not to
hurt their feet, and she tipped them back into the
jam jar.

"Twenty five . . . twenty six. . ." said Lulu.
"Twenty-seven! At last!"

"Whoever would have thought caterpillars could be such difficult pets?" said Nan.

"They don't mean to be difficult," said Lulu. "They just mean to be caterpillars. I suppose they're looking for a new patch of nettles. I wish we could find them one."

That was the problem.
There were no nettles
in Nan's garden.

There were no nettles
in Lulu's garden.

And there were not many in Mellie's or Charlie's
or Henry's garden.

No one could find a patch of nettles big enough
for twenty-seven caterpillars. They could only
find little bits.

"Well, nobody likes nettles," said Mellie.

"Except caterpillars," said Lulu.

The caterpillars loved nettles. They ate the leaves until they looked like nettle lace.

Every day they ate more and more and grew bigger and bigger.

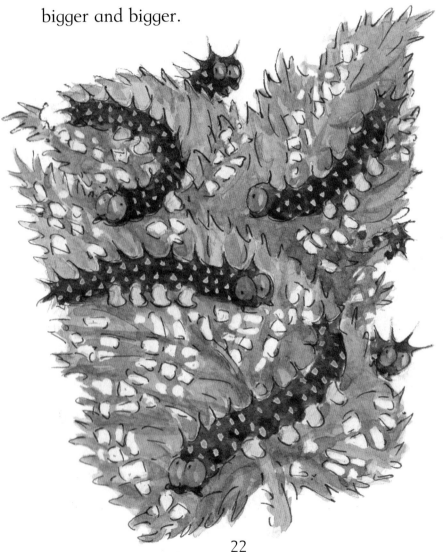

Lulu (in her winter gloves) picked nettles from the gardens of all of her friends.

"Please look after your nettle plants," she said to everyone. She wanted more nettles to grow.

Soon everyone knew about Lulu and nettles. They also knew about nettles and caterpillars.

"Caterpillars are AWFUL!" said Mellie.
"You've had them for ages and they're still not
tame. And they chew and chew and poo and poo
and get fatter and blacker and hairier.
Caterpillars are my worst things ever!"

"They're my best things ever," said Lulu.

Chapter Four

Mellie's birthday was coming and she was having a party. This was her first party ever. On all her other birthdays she had had Days Out.

Mellie gave Lulu a party invitation:

Please come to
my party!
Games in the garden
Picnic tea
Birthday sleepover
Cinema the
next day
And then
ice creams
in the park
if we're good

RSVP
AND VERY
IMPORTANT . . .

THIS IS A NO
CATERPILLAR
PARTY!

"I've waited all my life for a proper birthday party and I'm NOT having caterpillars!" said Mellie.

"I can't go to Mellie's birthday party because of my caterpillars," said Lulu to her family.

"Because of your caterpillars?" asked her mum.

"Because of your caterpillars?" asked her dad, and then they both looked at each other and said, "Because of her caterpillars???"

But Nan understood.

"I will look after the caterpillars," she said (she was a very brave nan). "You can't possibly miss Mellie's party!"

So the caterpillars went to Nan's house.

And Lulu went to the party.

And she never saw her twenty-seven hairy black caterpillars ever again.

Chapter Five

Nan felt terrible. She came round to Mellie's house and told them she felt terrible.

"Terrible!" she said.

Poor Mellie cried. She ate hot-air-balloon birthday cake and cried. "I wish I'd let your caterpillars come to my party. Then they wouldn't all be dead!"

That's what had happened to the caterpillars at Nan's house. They had stopped eating and eating and pooing and pooing. They had stopped being wriggly. Their hairiness had sagged. Their black had gone grey. They had crawled to dark places "and died," said Nan.

"But. . ." said Lulu.

"Oh!" said Mellie, getting tears on the icing.
"It's all my fault!"

"BUT. . ." said Lulu.

"Perhaps we should think again about getting that parrot?" asked Lulu's dad, and her mum said, "I always did say one day we should have a dog."

"BUT!" said Lulu. "SOMEBODY LISTEN! CATERPILLARS. . ."

"Have some
cake!" said Mellie,
passing her a chunk.

"LISTEN!" yelled
Lulu. "CATERPILLARS
DON'T DIE! THEY
TURN INTO
BUTTERFLIES!
EVERYONE KNOWS
THAT!"

"Oh my goodness!"
said Nan.

Nan's house was quiet when everyone arrived.
The giant-sized jam jar was empty in the bin.
But where were the nettles? Where were the
caterpillars?

"So as not to upset you," said Nan to Lulu, "my very nice neighbour took them away."

"WHICH very nice neighbour?" shouted Lulu.

Nan's very nice neighbour with the compost heap helped sort through the nettles on the top.

"Twenty five . . . twenty six. . ." counted Lulu and Mellie. "Twenty-seven! At last!"

Twenty-seven chrysalises in the box in Lulu's
bedroom.

Not dead.

Waiting.

Chapter Six

The chrysalises were waiting.

Lulu was waiting.

Mellie was waiting, and so was everyone else.

They waited for nearly twenty-seven days.
And then magic began.

Twenty-seven butterflies, Lulu's twenty-seven pets, flew away and left her.

Lulu watched them go.

"Twenty five, twenty six, twenty-seven!" she counted as she waved goodbye. "At last!"

"But what will happen now?"
asked Mellie.

"Well," said Lulu, "I do know
someone who says I can have
their parrot. And Mum says it's
really time this family had a dog.

Nan's very nice neighbour
is giving us a tortoise. And
guess what?. . .

Dad says there are nettles
growing back behind the
shed! So . . .
MORE CATERPILLARS!"